READING CHAMPION

The Best Crown Ever

by **Sue Graves** and **Farah Shah**

It was the king's birthday.

He was going to have a party.

"I want a crown for my party,"
said the king.
"I want the best crown ever!"

The king looked at
lots of crowns.

"This crown is too big,"
said the king.

"This crown is too small,"

said the king.

"This crown is too tall,"
said the king.

"This crown is too heavy,"

said the king.

The king was cross.

"I want the best crown ever!"

he shouted.

The queen looked at a cracker.

"We can pull this," she said.

"Here is your new crown!"

she said.

The king put on the crown.

It was not too big or too small.

It was not too tall or too heavy.

"It's the best crown ever!"
said the king.

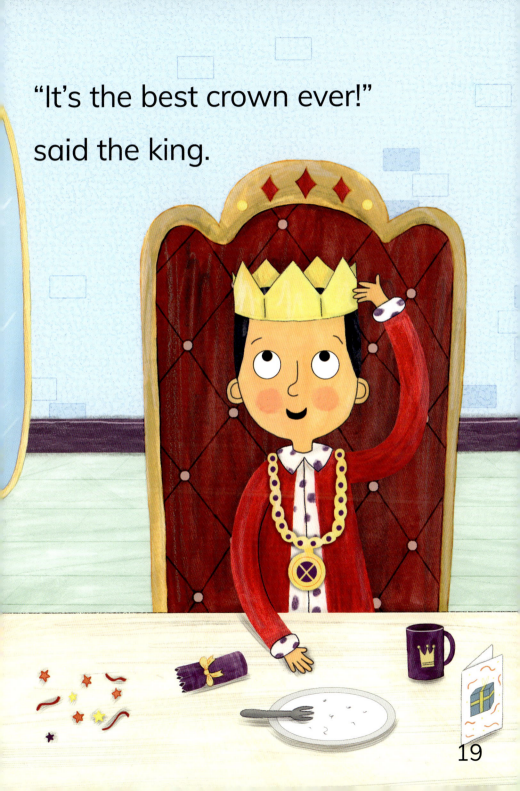

Story trail

Start

Start at the beginning of the story trail. Ask your child to retell the story in their own words, pointing to each picture in turn to recall the sequence of events.

Independent Reading

This series is designed to provide an opportunity for your child to read on their own. These notes are written for you to help your child choose a book and to read it independently.

In school, your child's teacher will often be using reading books which have been banded to support the process of learning to read. Use the book band colour your child is reading in school to help you make a good choice. *The Best Crown Ever* is a good choice for children reading at Blue Band in their classroom to read independently. The aim of independent reading is to read this book with ease, so that your child enjoys the story and relates it to their own experiences.

About the book
The king wants to wear the best crown ever for his party, but he just can't find the right one ...

Before reading
Help your child to learn how to make good choices by asking: "Why did you choose this book? Why do you think you will enjoy it?" Look at the cover together and ask: "What do you think the story will be about?" Support your child to think of what they already know about the story context. Read the title aloud and ask: "What is happening? Do you think the king likes the crown he is wearing?" Remind your child that they can try to sound out the letters to make a word if they get stuck.

Decide together whether your child will read the story independently or read it aloud to you. When books are short, as at Blue Band, your child may wish to do both!

During reading

If reading aloud, support your child if they hesitate or ask for help by telling them the word. Remind your child of what they know and what they can do independently. If reading to themselves, remind your child that they can come and ask for your help if stuck.

After reading

Support comprehension by asking your child to tell you about the story. Use the story trail to encourage your child to retell the story in the right sequence, in their own words.

Give your child a chance to respond to the story: "Did you have a favourite part? Which crown did you think was the best?"

Help your child think about the messages in the book that go beyond the story and ask: "Why do you think the king liked the crown at the end the best?"

Extending learning

Help your child understand the story structure by using the same sentence patterns and adding some new elements. "Let's make up a new story. The king is going to a party. He wants to wear the best robe ever, but none of them is right. What happens in your story?"

In the classroom, your child's teacher may be reinforcing punctuation and how it informs the way we group words in sentences. On a few of the pages, ask your child to find the speech marks that show us where someone is talking and read it aloud, making it sound like talking. Find the exclamation marks and ask your child to practise using appropriate expression.

Franklin Watts
First published in Great Britain in 2023
by Hodder & Stoughton

Series Editors: Jackie Hamley and Melanie Palmer
Series Advisors and Development Editors: Dr Sue Bodman and Glen Franklin
Series Designers: Cathryn Gilbert and Peter Scoulding

A CIP catalogue record for this book is
available from the British Library.

ISBN 978 1 4451 7437 2 (hbk)
ISBN 978 1 4451 7438 9 (pbk)
ISBN 978 1 4451 7471 6 (ebook)

Printed in China

Franklin Watts
An imprint of
Hachette Children's Group
Part of Hodder & Stoughton
Carmelite House
50 Victoria Embankment
London EC4Y 0DZ

An Hachette UK Company
www.hachette.co.uk

www.reading-champion.co.uk